Also by Bernard Jan

Memoir
A World Without Color

Novels
January River
Cruel Summer

Poetry
Postcards From Beyond Reality: The Selected Poems of Michael Daniels

LOOK FOR ME UNDER THE RAINBOW

Second revised edition

BERNARD JAN

BERNARD JAN

Look for Me Under the Rainbow

by

Bernard Jan

Published by Bernard Jan, Zagreb, 2018

Originally and first published in Croatian as *Potraži me ispod duge* by

Naklada Slon, Zagreb, 1993, ISBN 953-6203-01-4

The latest, fourth edition published in Croatian as *Potraži me ispod duge* by Katarina

Zrinski, Varaždin, 2015, ISBN 978-953-236-241-1

First published in English by Minerva Press, London, 1998,

ISBN 1-86106-831-X

Translated into English by Maja Šoljan and Bernard Jan

Editing and proofreading by Trish Reeb

Cover design by Mario Kožar MKM Media

Print On-Demand: amazon.com

ISBN (Print On-Demand) 978-953-59581-3-0

Cataloguing-in-Publication data available in the Online Catalogue of the National and
University Library in Zagreb under CIP record 000993837.

Contents

LOOK FOR ME UNDER THE RAINBOW 3

    The Ice-lover from Greenland 7

    The Wall of Death 49

    Rainbow Warriors 91

A NOTE FROM THE AUTHOR 111

ACKNOWLEDGEMENTS 119

SHARE WHAT YOU LOVE (ABOUT THE AUTHOR) . 121

REVIEWS 123

ACCLAIM FOR A WORLD WITHOUT COLOR 127

A WORLD WITHOUT COLOR EXTRACT 133

"All that is best in me I have given to (animals) and I mean to stand by them to the last and share their fate whatever it may be. If it is true that there is to be no haven of rest for them when their sufferings here are at an end, I, for one, am not going to bargain for any heaven for myself. I shall go without fear where they go, and by the side of my brothers and sisters from the forests and the fields, from skies to seas, lie down to merciful extinction in their mysterious underworld, safe from any further torments."

—Preface to *The Story of San Michele* by
Axel Munthe

"I have never been able to bring myself to extinguish a light of life; I lack the power to ignite it anew."

—Sven Hedin

LOOK FOR ME UNDER THE RAINBOW

"What is man, Mom?"

"Man's a great mystery. We know not where he comes from, nor where he's going. Elusive, like a shadow, he leaves wasteland in his wake."

"This . . . man, is he dangerous?"

"Very dangerous, son. You must try never to meet one. If you do come across man but it's too late to run, be brave. Wait for him. Whatever happens, never, ever turn your back on him. Look him straight in the eye. It's the only way you might save your life. That's the moment when he's most vulnerable and won't harm you."

"But how can I not meet a man? How do I avoid him?"

"You'll sense him coming close. You know, son, man has a special smell. The scent of fear, misfortune and pain. He feeds on it. You'll recognize him by this scent."

The Ice-lover from Greenland

The sea was unusually calm, even the deep currents seemed to stand still. As if suspended in the hushed stillness of dawn. The blue darkness of the night sky began to recede as the pale daylight washed over the horizon. Helped by the frail rays of the wintry sun shimmering through a cloud of fog. In the cold air, the coat woven out of the drops evaporated from the sea, turned into small crystals of ice.

The fog crept along the surface of the sea, dragging like a tired traveler, and spread in the direction of the land. Thin in places, thick in others, it occasionally revealed a glimpse of the blinding whiteness that covered most of the land.

If you looked at the right moment, when patches of fog dispersed enough to reveal an endless vista, you could see that it was, in fact, not land. Enveloped by the gradually disappearing fog, huge icebergs loomed, huddled atop the ice crust covering the sea of blue. At first glance, one might easily mistake them for a continent. It did, in fact, exist. The outline of the coast etched against the distant horizon was all part of nature's optical trick to fool a casual observer. Swathed in a mist of crystals, countless icebergs of various sizes stacked next to each other merged into the image of an ice mountain. The anomaly, carried by deep but weak currents, traveled the ocean almost imperceptibly.

If not for the sound of the icebergs clashing and breaking piercing the sleepy air, the entire scene would appear lifeless. A white wasteland. Even the scattered groups of seals dozing lazily on white sheets of ice, seemed motionless and almost unreal. Their dark, slick bodies struck a sharp contrast with the surrounding harmony of whiteness. As if they were unwanted intruders. Now and then a seal would move, usually a female. With a sharp sudden spasm, one cried out in pain struggling to bring a new life into this icy world of cruel beauty.

Having left her group, she lay on her side trying to find the most comfortable position to endure the labor pains. Growing stronger and more frequent, they produced searing pain. She felt the restless pup kick and strain to come out into a whole new world. A world of breathtaking beauty, yet fraught with danger. She wanted to help it. She matched the pace of her breathing with his efforts to break the thin membrane that divided him from the outer world. She synchronized her heartbeat with his, but to no avail.

She knew it was going to be a difficult birth. Still not full term, her offspring was in a hurry to leave her body. She nevertheless hoped the two of them would somehow succeed.

When the pup suddenly started to writhe and push inside her, she could not help howling in pain. Her cry resounded over the ice, eclipsing the muted groans of other mothers-to-be who were to begin labor in a few days. They were rested and ready, prepared for the hardship of giving birth, while she had only just arrived and was still exhausted after the long swim from the north. A journey she would again take several months from now with her pup, back home to the winter-bound land of eternal snow and ice. That is, *if* the birth went well and all ended happily.

As time went by, her fears seemed well founded. The last obstacle that separated her baby from the outer world was removed. Splashes of red blood stained the ice around her, slowly freezing in the bitter cold. But the pup still did not come. Not moving, exhausted and weary, it braced itself for another attempt.

She wondered whether it was male or female. If a male, would he look like his father who had just woken and proudly sniffed the air? If a female, would she, like her mother, one day have to go through this pain to bring her baby into the world? After carrying it lovingly inside her womb for months and months, only to. . . .

A new wave of excruciating pain slashed through her body and interrupted her thoughts. The pup pushed its way into the world, this time with more force and determination. The mother again synchronized all her bodily functions with its efforts to break free. Though united in their struggle, she wondered whether they felt the same pain. Or if only she suffered? Though it did not matter. She would gladly endure all the pain it took, if only to let it live.

As cry after piercing cry woke up other seals, they grew agitated, particularly the females about to become mothers in a few days. They timidly lifted their small heads to listen to the cries until they gradually abated. And then, one by one, they softly stretched on the ice that glistened in the sun. Silence fell, and everything was again hushed and motionless.

She could barely hold the overactive pup at her breast. He kept pulling away and refused to eat. His large black eyes squinted at the new surroundings with curiosity, blinking in the dazzling sunlight reflected from the white surfaces. Dark whiskers protruding from his snout combined with big chocolate eyes and two short hairs resembling antennae above each one, were all that disrupted the harmony of whiteness cloaking the pup. His fluffy fur, in its dreamlike softness once the afterbirth had been washed off, seemed to blend into the whiteness of the glacier. This fragile creature looked more like a chunk of white ice than a living being. Protected by nature like a mother shielding her baby from the perils that lurked.

His mother looked on tenderly as he gave in to her persistence and, something calmer, began to suckle. Content, she nevertheless remained on guard. Although seemingly relaxed, she'd primed her senses to detect the slightest of movements—any sign of danger or concealed threat. Her memories of the past, still too alive, filled her with a sense of foreboding.

The satiated pup stopped nursing and snuggled by his mother. But she could not get rid of the nameless fear. With one eye half-open, she eventually dozed, ready to snap awake at any sound.

She left him alone for a brief moment, to satisfy her

hunger. When she returned, the cub was nowhere to be found. *Nowhere!* She scanned the iceberg hoping to spot him, but in vain.

"Danny! Danny, where are you?"

Overcome by fear, she stumbled and slid over the smooth ice, searching for her son. She hoped he'd joined the other seals. When she saw he hadn't, she completely lost her head. She rushed forward, lurching and tripping, falling and rising again. Feverishly, she searched in each nook and cranny, turning at each shadow. Just when she thought it all over and lost hope of ever seeing him again, she saw something. On another end of the ice floe, a small and fluffy ball shuffled toward the sea.

"Danny!"

No reply. The chilly wind carried her voice away. Catching her breath, she dashed after her son still skidding toward the sea. She scurried over the ice with only enough strength to let out several sharp barks in succession. It seemed to work. The pup stopped for a moment and turned around. Giving his frantic mother time to catch him.

"Look, Mom! The sea!" He looked at her with shiny

button eyes.

"Come here, Danny, to Mommy! Let's go." Her heart pounding, she pressed him to her side and kissed the moist tip of his little nose.

"But, Mom, this is the sea." Eyes wide, the pup stared at the blue expanse of water stretching out between the giant icebergs into infinity.

"Yes, Danny, but you're too small to go in the water."

"When will I be able to go swimming?" Danny wailed.

"In a little while, after you grow up."

"When will that be?"

"Soon, my son." Smiling at his curiosity, she moved toward the center of the ice floe, holding him by the nape of his neck.

Forlorn, Danny watched adult seals slide off the glaciers and through the holes dug in the ice. They plunged into the water disappearing beneath the surface. Then briefly resurfaced to inhale the air before diving again in search of food or some underwater excitement.

Captivated, at first he didn't hear his mother speak to him.

"Danny?"

"Yes, mother," he said, yet felt a little ashamed as his thoughts wandered back to the icy cold seas.

"What have we learned today?" She looked at the pup waiting for his answer.

"That it's dangerous for baby seals to go into the water."

"Why is it dangerous for baby seals to go into the water, Danny?" she said, testing in detail his newly-acquired knowledge.

Danny finally managed to resist the magic call of the sea he'd listened to and obeyed without question. With a clear eye, he looked into his mother's eyes before he answered.

"Because they're still weak and inexperienced. And if they aren't careful, they could be dragged away by the current. Far away into the open sea where a dangerous killer whale may wait for a convenient moment to eat them up."

Mother seal looked adoringly at her son. He continued without a pause.

"They could also get lost, and not be able to find the way back to their family. They'd be alone, and hungry. If they fell into the water, the ice could cover them. Unable to emerge, they'd have no air and would choke and die. . . ."

He cocked his head adorned with thick fur. "Mom, what does it mean to die?"

She hugged the pup and murmured. "When I was small, just like you now, my mother held me close—like I'm holding you—and told me a wonderful story of Big Seal. Would you like to hear it, Danny?"

"Yes, tell it to me, Mom." The pup didn't give it a second thought. "Please?"

"All right. The story may be a short one, but it's enlightening. I hope you like it as much as I do. It offered me comfort and warmth while I grew up experiencing both good and bad moments in my life. The memories I cherish and the ones I try to forget.

"This story's about Big Seal born many, many years ago. Long before any of us. And the first seal to come into this world, but nobody knows exactly how or when. However, he didn't come alone. He had a faithful companion, his wife. Big Seal lived a long life, had many sons and daughters—more than you can see here now—and died of old age. When he felt death approaching and realized he'd have to leave behind the seas and coasts he loved, he gathered all the seals around him. He announced the time had come for him to depart from them as well as this world. All the seals began to grieve and weep. Their sorrow omnipresent, their warm tears flooded the sea and green coasts. The water started to turn into little ice cubes. With so many, soon the entire landscape started to turn cold. The sea froze in places, thus giving birth to the icebergs of tears.

"Seeing the unhappiness and pain caused by his words, Big Seal tried to comfort the other seals. He told them not to be afraid or sad. Although they'd never see him again, he'd always remain with them. He promised: *Before I go, I shall give you something to remember me by. I shall paint a rainbow in the sky. When you see it, think of me. Each one of you will see a rainbow. But only once in your lifetime will you see your own. And when you see your rainbow, you'll know the time has come to bid farewell and leave. You'll feel it. Then you must swim to the end of your rainbow. It'll be in the clearest and cleanest sea. You'll pick your favorite of its colors. If you succeed in climbing and reaching that color of the rainbow, you'll know you were a good seal who loved his brothers and sisters. And when you see the sun on top of the rainbow and beneath it the coasts full of flowers like they were before your tears turned them to ice, call me and I'll come to take you to the Big Land."*

"What's the Big Land?" Danny said.

"The Big Land is much like this world we live in now only more beautiful. And bigger. The seas clearer than tears, are filled with fish. Glaciers rise all the way to the sky where there's always a rainbow. The Big Land has room for all the seals that ever lived. And for us living now as well as those who come after."

"Will there be flowers and green coasts, too, like before the seals started to weep?"

"Yes, and warmer seas crisscrossing with cold underwater currents will be our signposts to the colder seas. Glaciers, more beautiful and safe than the ones here, will adorn them."

"It sounds wonderful!" Danny said breathless.

"It is, son. But the tale of Big Seal isn't finished. Telling this to the seals, Big Seal bid them goodbye and went alone to a solitary iceberg. Soon after, icy rain began to fall and the sun came out. A multi-colored rainbow appeared in its center and arched down to the sea. The eldest son went to look for Big Seal, but he'd disappeared. Soon the magnificent rainbow vanished as well."

"What does a rainbow look like, Mom?"

"The most beautiful sight imaginable. Soft colors merge to create an airy arch across the sky."

"If it's made of air, how can we climb it?"

"Remember, Big Seal said only good seals will succeed."

"And the rest?" Danny said with trepidation. "Has it ever happened that a seal couldn't climb the rainbow?"

"As far as I know, all of them succeeded."

"This means some day we'll do it, too?"

"If we're good." She smiled at him. "We certainly will, Danny."

*

A commotion among the seals interrupted their lesson. Danny and his mother turned to see from where the loud barks came. A young seal in another group came to their ice floe and challenged Danny's father with powerful bellows that echoed across the ice. A merciless fight broke out but, fortunately for the young rebellious seal, it lasted only a short while. Puffing up his chest and releasing a victorious howl, Danny's father looked on as the young seal he successfully overpowered beat a swift retreat into the safety of the sea.

"Dad is so big and strong," Danny said. "You know, Mom, I want to be just like him when I grow up."

"You will if you listen and learn, Danny," his mother said. "Now, where were we?"

"The storm."

"And what about it?"

"If we're in the water and notice a storm coming, we must . . . Mom?"

"What is it now, Danny?"

"Is only the sea dangerous? Is there anything on the ice we should watch out for and fear?"

With an imperceptible shiver, Danny's mother stared into the distance.

"Yes, son, there are dangerous things here, too."

"Like what?"

"The greatest danger is the polar bear. They know how to travel on icebergs and, if we aren't careful, they can surprise us."

"Are there any polar bears on these ice floes?" Danny trembled.

"Not on ours." She managed a weak smile, although her mind was in turmoil with dark thoughts.

"How do you know? Are you sure?"

"Your father and other leaders searched these ice floes carefully before we settled here."

"So I don't have to worry about the polar bear!" Danny let out his breath. "Are there other dangers?"

"The other danger—"

Voices and shouts, clearer and closer, boomed hollowly inside her head.

"Mom!"

Voiceless cry, eyes frozen with tears, pain and lack of understanding. Blood.

"Mom!"

"The other danger's man," she panted out with effort. The same effort she tried to bottle up her memories, but without success.

"Man?" Danny scratched his head.

He'd never heard this word and didn't know what to think.

"What is man, Mom?"

Dull thuds from all directions, blood splattered the white carpet of ice, oozing, coagulating in the cold.

"Mom . . ." he nudged his mother with his nose. "Mom, what happened?"

"Nothing, Danny, it's nothing." She kissed the tiny creature clinging to her. "My thoughts wandered. What did you ask me?"

"I asked, what is man?"

She gently rested her head on his and closed her eyes. She breathed deeply in and out and clouds of warm air came out of her trembling nostrils.

"Man. . . . Man's a great mystery. We know not where he comes from, nor where he's going. Elusive, like a shadow, he leaves wasteland in his wake. Wasteland and destruction."

"This . . . man, is he dangerous?"

"Very dangerous, son. More than anything you can imagine or will ever see in your life. You must try never to meet one. If you do come across man but it's too late to run, be brave. Wait for him. Whatever happens, never, ever turn your back on him. Look him straight in the eye. It's the only way you might save your life. That's the moment when he's most vulnerable and won't harm you. Human beings attack on the sly, behind your back."

"But how can I not meet a man? How do I avoid him?" the pup said, his tone hopeless.

"You'll sense him coming. You know, son, man has a special smell. The scent of fear, misfortune, and pain. He feeds on it. You'll recognize him by this scent."

*

The crystal clear and cloudless blue sky stretched in an endless expanse—its borders, invisible and distant. Gusts of cold and sharp breeze disturbed the clarity that turned the entire landscape into something unearthly.

Giant icebergs scattered over the sea. Their ragged peaks jutted into the skyline toward the distant sun, threatening to extinguish it forever. The sun shot its fiery rays downward, slowly melting the ice on the crags and blunting their menacing points. Tiny drops of water gleamed in the sunlight. Only to freeze in the next instant when the ray slightly weakened or changed its angle.

At first glance, this icy world appeared dead and barren. Yet daily, life proliferated all around. New pups were born every day covering entire ice floes with their flat little fur-coated bodies.

Danny watched with joy as baby seals crawled out from hollows in the ice that served as cots and waddled to their mothers. They hungrily suckled on warm milk before returning to their ice beds to continue their sleep.

Danny's seemingly indifferent father strutted around

their group, protecting them from unexpected enemies. Now and then he emitted a proud bellow. The sight not far from him was in every faction full of love; Danny could hardly stop himself from running to join them. He wanted to snatch some of that warm intimacy for himself, as well as play with the new pups. He wished he could get closer to his father too. Though he reached out to him several times, his father treated him with such aloofness Danny backed off—ashamed and aching. Alone. Back to the loneliness in which he spent the first eight days of his life, because his mother would still not let him join the others.

"But, Mom, why aren't we living with other seals? Why are we alone? Why can't I play with the others? Look how happy they are!" He watched with longing as two pups rolled down the icy slope, playfully holding each other by the neck.

"Be patient, son," his mother always replied. "Soon you will be able to play with them, too."

"But when, Mom, when?"

"Soon, Danny, very soon."

And this ended the conversation. Over, before it

even started.

Although sad and disappointed, he did not protest. He knew his mother had her reasons for not letting him move about freely and play with the other young seals. Since she promised his solitary *imprisonment* would not last long, he did not think about it anymore. After all, his mother loved him more than anything else in the world. He knew she would never deliberately harm him. So, he accepted this penance. Even though he did not understand, it must be for his own good.

One day everything changed. Danny got a brother. Overwhelmed with joy, he completely forgot about the fear he felt when his mother left him alone a little longer than usual. He had begun to think something happened to her. Like maybe the sea current dragged her to the open sea where a killer whale swallowed her up . . . or a shark tore her apart . . . or she got caught in the ice . . . or she met a man. . . . But when he saw her coming with a tiny pup in tow, just opening its eyes, his fears and foreboding dispelled.

Danny received Jon with such sincere affection and love, his mother almost burst into tears from happiness and pride.

Jon's mother died in labor leaving him alone. And he barely survived.

Even Danny's father, in their vicinity at that moment, was slightly bemused by this extraordinary show of affection. But as soon as Danny—feeling his gaze—turned to look at him, his father averted his eyes and disappeared behind a huge chunk of ice.

Now she had not one, but two pups to worry about. Danny refused to be weaned and now Jon suckled as if he had not tasted food in his entire life. Still, Danny's mother knew she did the right thing. Her malcontent and mischievous little pup Danny whom she could not let out of sight even for a second, now changed beyond recognition. Not only did he stop pestering her with his interminable questions, he almost stopped his *excursions* to the sea. His attention focused on Jon, he treated his adopted brother with warmth and kindness. She thought that was amazing. If she weren't a mother who loved Danny more than anything in the world, she might have thought his love for Jon stronger than her own. But that was impossible. She loved Danny as much as it was possible to love anybody.

For Danny, these were the happiest moments of his young life. Though much more free to roam as he wished, he never abused his mother's trust. As the day when he would be granted independence swiftly approached and the call of the deep grew stronger, he didn't mind waiting a little longer. With his love for Jon, the most important thing in his life, everything else became secondary.

Shards of ice flew into the air and clouds of white crystalline dust rose around the two rivals locked in battle. The ice floe trembled with the heat of the fight, their fierce barks and roars echoed between the icebergs disappearing in the distance. Narrow creeks of blood ran down the bodies of tired opponents, and bites and scratches adorned as trophies their fat skin.

The fight seemed to subside as the challenger gathered strength for a new attack on his much older but more experienced rival.

Folding his back flippers under his body and raising himself as tall as possible, Danny's father prepared to deal with the young rebel slowly circling around him. With a roar, the young seal came at him. The duel resumed. The circle around the rivals widened, leaving them enough space to fight it out until the final victory. Or defeat.

Danny and Jon watched the duel from an elevation that gave them an excellent view. With awe and respect, they observed the older seal standing his ground, successfully resisting attacks from the young, now very angry male. But also with fear. The wounds on the older seal's body, particularly his neck, bled profusely. But he held up. In fact, in the last few clashes he gradually gained an advantage. He charged powerfully at the youngster who knew he was losing the battle. And that he would ultimately have to surrender. Now he only wanted to leave the battlefield with at least a semblance of dignity. Once before he had been forced to beat a shameful retreat. He did not like the idea of that happening again. But his older opponent did not show him mercy. No way would he get out of this duel without losing face. The youngster kept charging back until finally he had to admit defeat.

He stood making low grunting noises. Although the match had been fair, he could not reconcile himself to the fact a much older seal defeated him. Avoiding the eyes of other seals, he crawled over the ice toward a far corner where he could hide and be alone with his pain and wounded pride.

Reaching the top of the slope, the rebel found himself face to face with a pup—the only seal who did not move to make way. Loudly growling, his rage and frustration boiling over, he warned Danny to move. Not afraid, he regarded the young male without making a sound. The youngster lost control and threw himself at Danny. But before he made contact, he felt the ice shake beneath his body. Something hit him, throwing him in the air and sending him rolling off the iceberg. His body crashed against the ragged edge of the ice. He stared at the old seal standing beside his son before the sea pulled the poor loser under and closed above his head, swallowing him forever.

Hard to tell who was more surprised and taken aback—father or son. While the somewhat confused father breathing heavily with bleeding wounds stood beside his small, frail son, Danny caught a glimpse of his dad's eyes—and saw something he never expected. His father's expression rewarded Danny with a gift of love and admiration he waited days to receive. The older seal's bark as he greeted the shining sun again, emphasized the moment.

"Danny, can you look after Jon until I return?"

"Of course, Mom. You don't have to worry at all." He winked at his younger brother.

"Please, be careful, boys."

She still remembered the raging seal charging at

Danny and almost crushing him to death.

"You can play whatever you like, but don't go near water and don't wander off too far. If there's any trouble, you'll find shelter here. And call me immediately in case of danger. I'll hear you."

"Don't you worry, Mom."

"Jon, be a good boy and listen to Danny." The little pup looked up at her with love.

She knew she was an overly anxious and protective mom even though Danny had behaved responsibly lately. Plus, Jon was a good, quiet pup any mother would have wished for her own.

"Yes, Mom." He blinked and slightly cocked his head.

To some extent reassured, she smiled at them and went off to search for food.

"Remember, if you need me. . . ."

As soon as she said that, she dove under the water.

"What would you like to play, Jon?"

"Hide-and-seek!" Jon jumped for joy.

"All right, then! I'll look for you first."

Danny barely managed to finish the sentence and

Jon already sped across the ice toward the slope.

"Don't go too far!" Danny yelled after him, and laughed.

"I won't." Jon scuttled behind a huge block of ice.

Danny waited a bit to give Jon enough time to hide, and then began to move in the same direction. He checked each corner along the way, even turning small chunks of ice with his nose. Aware the younger pup watched him from his hiding place pleased that Danny could not find him, he wanted to let Jon enjoy it as long as possible. Although the older seal's sharp eyes soon discerned a white furry ball huddled behind a pile of broken ice, he pretended not to notice. He continued his search moving in circles around his little brother. When the game seemed long enough, Danny quietly snuck up behind Jon's back. While feigning fatigue and sulking because of his failure, he said in a cracked voice, "Ah-ha, here you are! You could have hidden even better so I wouldn't find you until Mom came back. That's what you wanted, right?"

"You couldn't find me, you couldn't find me!" The little seal skipped up and down, flapping his flippers.

"But I found you after all! It took me a little longer, but I finally did it," Danny said pretending indignation.

"You couldn't see me, could you?" Jon cheerfully pushed him with his nose.

"All right, I couldn't see you," Danny said softly, "but now it's your turn to look for me. Let's see how well you do."

He gently pushed Jon in the direction of the huge block of ice. When he turned his back, Danny called, "Are your eyes closed?"

"Yes."

"I'm going now. You can come after me when you've counted twenty seals. Did you hear me?"

"Yes, yes!" Jon said.

Danny slowly padded over to the edge of the ice block and, turning to Jon, halted. He watched him count fast—one seal, two seals, four seals, six . . .—and then called out, "Are your eyes closed?"

"Closed!" Jon squinted with one eye. Then he continued counting.

"Eight seals, nine seals, eleven seals. . . ."

Danny laughed and slid across the ice.

"Twelve seals, thirteen seals, fifteen seals. . . ."

Passing their shelter, Danny headed to a group of seals. Let him find me now, if he can, Danny thought and disappeared into the crowd.

Mother heard a commotion on the ice floe. She took a break in the hunt. Giving up on the fish she almost grabbed, she swam to the surface. First she saw Danny peering into the crevices in the ice, and then her eyes searched for Jon. The group of seals still sunned themselves with only a few jumping into the water. She sniffed the air again. Suspicious, the mom rolled over the edge of the ice floe and plunged into the depths.

Swift as a flash of lightning and graceful, she ripped the water chasing a frightened fish. Arching her body with two or three powerful thrusts of her flippers, she intercepted it and snatched it into her mouth. A moment later, she swam after the dispersing school of fish.

Mother came to the surface several times to get some

air and to see what the little ones were up to. She saw Jon looking for something and realized they played hide-and-seek, their favorite game. Jon must be having a really hard time now, she knew, as he always did when he had to find well-hidden Danny. She felt sorry for the youngest, but could not help him with his search because she had to find the runaway fish. She dove in, but a strange feeling of anxiety clutched at her heart.

Just as she started to chase and catch up to her prey, she heard a deafening rumble and felt the ice above her tremble. Petrified, she listened to the strident screech of breaking ice. With swift movements, she swam to the hole in the ice from which she surfaced a few minutes ago.

Sliding, stumbling, she managed to climb onto the ice floe. She looked in the direction of the barking group of seals, at the same time they plunged into the sea. Fear and panic spread to other groups. Almost in an instant, all disappeared. Only the unprotected young remained behind on the empty ice floes.

Her blood ran cold when she looked at the place where her boys were supposed to be. Nobody there. No sign of life. With tears in her eyes, she uttered a bark full of pain and anguish.

"Danny! Jon!"

"Danny? Don't do this to me! Where are you?" Jon said. He had already searched everywhere and found no trace of his brother. Ready to give up and admit defeat, he remembered something. Of course! The only place he had not checked, their shelter. He must have hidden there. He thought Jon would not find him, but Jon was not a stupid seal. How funny it would be to see his brother's surprised face.

Curled among the pups, Danny observed Jon in the distance searching the iceberg. He heard his bleat and call, pointing his nose upward. He stood like this for a while, waiting, and then continued to look for his brother. Danny smiled and assumed an even more comfortable position. *Look, Jon, look, maybe you'll even find me.*

The seals became agitated. Afraid he'd be discovered, Danny cautiously lifted his little head and peered around. Aside from muffled barks and several adult seals diving into the sea, he noticed nothing unusual. He crouched again, his eyes following Jon, now hurrying to their shelter.

Suddenly a strange sensation he never felt before coursed through his body. The ice trembled under him and loud barking and howls pierced the air. The serenity and silence interrupted, seals plunged into the sea. Danny looked around, puzzled, unable to grasp what was going on. Lying in the middle of other baby seals, he saw something resembling a huge cliff covered with ice appear behind an iceberg. Even when it moved toward him, in his confusion, he still could not figure out what was happening. He simply stared at the strange apparition and even stranger creatures moving with it.

At first he thought it some kind of unfamiliar iceberg. He had never seen anything like these extraordinary creatures that moved on hind legs only. Fascinated, he paid little attention to the rainbow captured in brilliant colors on the side of the strange green iceberg. He also failed to notice much about the white bird—the white bird beneath the rainbow holding a twig in its beak. Unfamiliar with this species, he could not remember his mother ever telling him anything about such a creature. But it did not matter. All his attention was focused on the strange creatures dismounting from their iceberg and starting to mill about the ice.

In shock, he gazed at a funny-colored figure running toward the group of frightened pups who clung to each other calling for help. He could not take his eyes off the creature, its upper body red and lower gray. Nor could he move. Shivering in terror, he waited for whatever would happen.

"Danny!" He suddenly heard a voice calling him.

He turned to his mother loudly bleating and, scared

to death, rushing over to him.

"Run, Danny, this is *man*!"

His body shook all over with the terrifying knowledge. He recalled his mother's warnings and the fear they instilled in him. Now real, he felt the palpable presence of man reaching the first pups and doing something terrible to them.

"Danny!"

His mother's voice finally prodded him into action. He rushed toward her with all his might—at least he thought so. In fact, he crawled slowly and helplessly.

Once more he heard his mother's voice telling him to hurry. He looked back to see what the man did and almost fainted from fear. All the pups were dead! Their furry bodies soaked in green blood. The human being guilty of this stood up and, noticing Danny, started after him.

Too late, Danny realized he did not have time nor strength enough to reach his mother for protection. With tears in his eyes, he watched her blurred shape stumbling slowly closer to him and tried to call out. But he could not, his throat felt choked. He braced himself for what was coming.

Trying not to turn away, he looked the human in the eyes, at least he thought those were the eyes of this bizarre creature. He had learned the lesson well, as everything else his mother taught him, and now he had to apply his knowledge in real life whether he liked it or not. Staring, he stood motionless even when he heard noises behind him. In the corner of his field of vision, he noticed his mother between him and the human being. She growled dangerously even when the thing covering the creature's head fell off as it slipped onto the ice in its effort to go around his mother. Danny's fear disappeared, when he saw something almost unbelievable.

Lovely golden hair, soft as the finest fur, fell in waves down the red buttoned-up parka. Danny thought it must be human fur. He couldn't stop gazing at the sea colored eyes, set in the perfectly carved features of her face. They caressed him with pleasant warmth and kindness. Only red lips, the tip of the nose and rosy cheeks stood in contrast to the harmony and beauty of the face.

When she sprayed his fur and spoke words he did not understand, Danny was not afraid. At the same time, she held his mother at a safe distance, not allowing her to come closer. He could do nothing but stare at those eyes, the incredible blue eyes that came from an unknown world. Enchanted, he looked at his own image reflected in them while she gently patted his head, whispering tenderly. She stood up, folded her hair back under the hood, smiled at him and started back to the ship from which she had come and scared the wits out of him. And Danny still looked at her, transfixed. His mother's tears, falling like warm and silent drops on his face, returned him to reality.

"My son, what have they done to you?" she wailed, sniffing his fur now covered in vivid green patterns. "What have they done?"

"Don't cry, Mom, I'm fine. I'm all right." He looked at the other pups green from head to paddles no longer frozen in fear, as they began to cry and shuffle along the ice. "Nothing terrible happened."

"But, Danny, your fur. . . . Look at yourself! What have they done to your fur? How are we going to wash it off?"

She glanced in a direction of the pups, bright green

against the white ice, and sighed deeply. "Whatever has happened to us?"

"You know, Mom," Danny feigned timidity, while in reality trying to be considerate to his mother, "I almost like it this way."

"Nonsense, child!" His mother was shocked.

"I like my fur this way. Now I feel . . . I don't know how to say it, really, but I think I feel safer."

"Safer? Now you stick out for miles!"

"That's why, Mom! Because if I am ever again in danger, it'll be much easier for you to spot me and come to my rescue!" He smiled at his beaming mother. "The only thing I'm sorry for is that I won't be able to play hide-and-seek with Jon anymore," he added when he saw Jon, who had mustered courage and come out of their shelter looking at Danny with his mouth fallen open.

"Oh, Danny, when will you grow up?" His mother looked at him, but this time her gaze was a bit different than usual.

"Soon, Mom, very soon." He recognized in his mother's eyes the shape of a now already grown up seal.

Radiating with joy because of their understanding, he smiled at her once again. And then he started toward Jon waiting for him, impatient and white as snow.

Light as a snowflake dancing in the air, he hovered, soared high. Thrilled to float higher and higher. Smooth and effortless. Think it and you are already lifting.

That moment stretched into eternity. Then burst and disintegrated. Bathed in sunlight, like the white dove that flew above him carrying a twig in her beak, it was the last thing Danny saw, before meeting his rainbow.

The Wall of Death

Everything ready for the long trip further north, the sea teemed with thousands of seals. Their barks resounded across the surface. They traveled in a large group. Adults led the way. The youngsters, born this spring, trailed behind as if reluctant to leave the ice floes where they first saw the light of the world. And lived sixteen weeks of their lives. The place where they acquired the necessary knowledge to survive, caught their first fish from this sea with an abundance of them . . . and saw human beings.

The other seals had traveled quite a distance, but Danny still stood on the edge of the ice floe, staring at the landscape he became so fond of in his brief life. He loved the icebergs, the sea, the ice floe where he and Jon played hide-and-seek. And he'd never forget the moment he laid his eyes on her—the human female. Overwhelmed by the memories of the past weeks, he held back. They made it hard for him to decide to embark on the long migration. Though the call of his homeland was equally powerful, if Jon had not asked in a gentle voice, "Shall we go, Danny?" he was sure he would have stayed. Leaving them to wander this icebound world and beautiful sea for a year, while they waited for their group to return.

A dream that could not come true, Danny knew it well. He smiled at his younger brother. "Let's go, Jon. We're already late."

Jon dove straight into the sea. Tossing his head to shake off the water drops, he called Danny to join him. Danny stretched his short neck as much as he could, raised his nose to the pale sky and let out a loud bark. Then he plunged into the sea and headed for his homeland.

*

"What is Greenland, Mom?"

"It's the place your ancestors came from, Danny."
She smiled gently at Jon hanging on her every word.
"Your grandfathers and grandmothers, your father, me,
even Jon and you."

"How can I be from Greenland when I was born
here?"

"I was born here, too, and so was your father, on
these same ice floes."

"Here on these ice floes?" Jon's eyes went wide.

"No, Jon, it's just a way of putting it. We always return to this part of the world, but the group never stays
on the same ice floe twice."

"Why?"

"Because that's impossible. Even if we wanted to, we
wouldn't be able to find the exact ice floes. They change
in time, just as we do. The old ones disappear, new ones
are born, some break and turn into several small ice
floes, and even those that remain unchanged are not the

same. Everything changes in a special way. Besides, it wouldn't be safe to stay always at the same place."

"Why wouldn't it be safe?" asked Danny.

"Danny, have you forgotten what I taught you?"

"No, Mom, I haven't, but—"

"We won't discuss it again, all right?"

He wrinkled his nose to express his dissatisfaction, but as always obeyed his mother. "Okay, Mom, we won't talk about it, if you say so."

He resented that she dismissed his favorite subject so abruptly. He wanted to learn more about human beings, but his mother's reply stayed the same. She would not give in to him. Even when he pointed out that man wasn't all that bad. The nice human female had not hurt him at all. She even smiled and stroked his fur, but his mother refused to change her opinion. She reminded him that, if nothing else, the human female did ruin his fur. And regardless of everything, he must stay away from human beings because sooner or later it would be a matter of survival. *Man is man*, she'd say, *and while he may change his skin, the character remains the same.*

In no hurry to get to Greenland, Danny swam next

to Jon at the rear of the group. In fact, if anybody were to ask him, he would say he wished to set out in the opposite direction, to the south where his human female headed. But no one asked. All the beauties of Greenland his mother described seemed pale in comparison to the dazzling human. He hoped to see her again next year when the group returned to these parts. He wanted to know her better.

"Danny, let's race!" Jon jumped out of the water.

"You're on. The first to reach the rear end of the main group is the winner."

"But, Danny, isn't that a bit too far?"

Danny only smiled. "Ready, steady, go!"

He left a foamy trail in the water behind him along with Jon, paddling as fast as he could to catch up.

"Ugh, some race." Jon sprawled on the ice floe. "I didn't think we'd make it."

"Just stick to me, pal, and we'll swim across the seas

of this world. We'll explore all ice floes, even those at Greenland. When there's nothing left to explore, we'll go south. Only you and me." Danny added softly, "Where man lives."

"If Mom heard this, she wouldn't like it, Danny." Jon looked at the other seals who were about to continue their journey after a short rest. "She'd be very sad."

"Don't worry, Jon, she won't be if we don't tell her. Anyway, I'm joking."

"Besides, men are up north, too."

But not her, Danny wanted to say, but changed his mind.

"Are you hungry, Jon?"

"No, just a little tired."

"You stay here and rest. I'll catch some food for us."

"Shouldn't we be taking off too?" Anxious, Jon glanced at the empty ice and tiny dots in the distance traveling north.

"We'll go as soon as we've eaten something. And you need to rest for the next race."

Danny dived into the water, fresh as if he just woke up after several hours of sleep.

*

For the next few days, Danny and Jon continued to travel north in this unusual fashion. Occasionally they stayed so far behind they didn't see the group at all, not even the weakest seals bringing up the rear. Thus, they followed their instincts. Sometimes they hurried almost to the edge of the main group to join the adult seals. This caused a flurry of disapproval for their playful pranks. Now and then they saw their mother, but soon lost sight of her. Sometimes when others rested, the pair veered off course to explore strange and forbidden seas. But their unerring instinct always led them in the right direction. North.

"Danny, do you imagine Greenland looks the way Mother described it? Countless islands of ice stretching all the way to the steep cliffs of the coast where many birds make their nests?"

"And where fat polar bears walk, just waiting for the

right moment to catch you!" added Danny.

"With nights long and light, like daytime. And up there, in the farthest north, they will go on endlessly, the sun never rising or setting, as if time stopped. As if everything ceases, clad in whiteness and bound in ice. Aren't you looking forward to the fragrance of polar night and the beautiful sights?" Jon said, with a gleam in his eyes.

"You know, Jon, I thought it was beautiful where we were. Even the nights, although much shorter and darker, were filled with beauty. And the sea, blue and rich with fish, seemed somehow friendlier and nicer than where we swim now. If this is how it looks, I must tell you, I've no desire to see the famous Greenland."

"You're right, the sea does seem a little strange lately. I noticed that myself. As we go further we see more of these shiny specks on the water. They look like plankton, but they're oily! Yuck! Have you noticed how disgusting they taste?"

"You haven't been eating them, Jon, have you?"

"No, but one floated into my mouth when I came to the surface. You try it. You've never tasted anything so disgusting in your life!"

"No, thank you, fish are good enough for me."

"For me, too. At least, they were, but I wonder if it's going to stay that way."

Jon grew despondent.

"What do you mean?"

"Haven't you noticed the farther we travel, the less fish there are and more difficult to find? It's been that way since the oily specks first appeared. And the fish we caught . . . just gave themselves over, as if waiting for someone to catch them. Like they didn't feel like running away or racing against us."

"It only seemed that way. Even if it were true, it's probably temporary. Things will improve in time," Danny said.

"I hope you're right. Listen, Danny, how far behind the others are we? I can't seem to find my bearings."

"They can't be too far away. Are you tired? Would you like to take a break?"

"No. I'm not tired. Only . . . only a little uncertain."

"What do you mean, *uncertain*?"

"Well . . . Danny, are you positive we're swimming in the right direction?"

"Positive? Of course I'm positive! Why wouldn't I be?"

"No reason, I'm only asking."

"Come on, Jon, lighten up. Can't you feel the fragrance of the polar night coming closer and calling out to us?"

But this time Jon said nothing.

"Danny?!"

"What is it?"

Danny swam to the surface and looked where Jon pointed.

"Look! What is it?"

"What?"

"There, in front of us! That large stain! It's moving toward us!"

"Take it easy, Jon, it's only the sea."

"But there's something on the surface!"

"Maybe there is and maybe there isn't," Danny said.

"Maybe the sea up north is just different from our sea."

"Are you sure?"

"I don't know," Danny shook his head, "but we'll find out soon." He swam with fast strokes toward the rapidly growing stain.

"Jon? Jon!" Danny looked around in terror.

He heard Jon's voice say, "What happened?"

"Where are you?"

"Here, right beside you," came Jon's voice again.

"Where *here*?" Danny turned in the direction of the familiar bark. "Jon, what happened to you? You're black as soot!"

"What happened to *me*? Look at yourself! You don't look any better."

It was true. Stunned, Danny realized his beautiful silvery-gray fur was coated in an oily, sticky substance. And it didn't go away when he tried to remove it with his nose.

"Jon, something's strange going on here." Danny watched his brother with growing concern. "I think we'd better get out of this thing, whatever it is."

"But, how are we going to do that? It seems endless!"

"Hold on, let's think about it. We've been caught in this black stain for quite a while now, haven't we? Since this isn't the sea, better to say not *only* the sea, but something floating on the surface, it must have an end somewhere, just as it had a beginning. Therefore, we must only continue to swim and sooner or later the stain will be gone."

"Swim where, Danny?"

"Toward these icebergs. To the north."

"What icebergs?"

"The ones before us."

"Or maybe the ones behind us." Jon shook his head. "Danny, do you have any idea what's ahead and what's behind us? Do you know where north is? I sincerely hope you do, because I haven't got a clue!"

*

"I can't go on, Danny. I'm dead tired. I can't even catch fish, let alone fight my way through this black stain."

"Must admit I don't feel too great myself. We'll stay here on this ice floe for a while to rest. Who knows, if we're lucky, the current will carry us."

"Wish I knew where our group is now," Jon said. "How far they've gone. . . . Will we ever reach them, Danny? Since this happened to us, I've completely lost hope that we'll meet up again. I can't recognize myself. I don't know. . . . I don't know how to explain it, but I'm not myself. I feel . . . lost. If it weren't for you, Danny. . . ."

"Come on, Jon, everything's going to be fine, you'll see. We just need some rest. A good night's sleep and things will look better. I'm sure about that."

"It's just the sight of this sea makes it all seem so hopeless. I can't imagine how we'll get out. Why didn't Mom warn us about these stains, Danny? Why didn't she tell us they were dangerous and that we should watch out for them? We wouldn't be in this trouble and lost if she'd told us."

"It's not Mom's fault, Jon. Maybe she didn't even know they existed. And as for being lost, that's not true. Once we are out of the stain, we'll continue on our journey."

"Where to, Danny?"

"Home, to Greenland."

"And how, if I may ask?" His wariness reflected in Jon's eyes.

"By smell. We'll follow the smell of our ancestors."

"Forgive me, please, but lately I've smelled only one thing. And this smell, I just cannot believe there's something so, so . . . crude!"

"All right, I admit our sense of smell has deteriorated a bit, but don't forget the stars and the sun. We'll follow them." Danny sounded adamant.

"What stars, what sun? Have you seen the sky lately? It's gray, as in a nightmare!"

"Stop it, Jon, stop pestering and go to sleep." Danny rolled over. "Once we've had some sleep, everything will be different, I promise."

*

Danny kept his promise, not knowing himself how that actually happened. When they woke up, they didn't know where to look. Everything, from one end of the horizon to the other was covered by whiteness. That included themselves, the ice floe on which they rested, and the stain that had captured the sea. Only the icy peaks of surrounding icebergs were visible in the magnificent, almost frightening, landscape.

"Danny, what do you think, how long will this last?"

"What?"

"The storm."

"I don't know. It seems to have just started."

Danny was right again. The dense tiny ice crystals filled the air and they could barely see each other. The blasting wind, growing stronger every second, howled over the sea.

"Danny?"

"What is it, Jon?"

"Can I cuddle next to you?"

"Sure. Of course."

The ice cracked in the freezing cold and the wind raged into a storm, sweeping everything in its way. But Danny and Jon were not aware of it. They slept huddled together, dreaming of Greenland.

Jon shivered.

"Danny!"

"Yes?" he said half-asleep.

"I wish Mom were here."

"So do I."

"I miss her a lot."

A strong gust of wind blinded them with a spray of icy dust.

"Jon, are you asleep?"

"No, I can't sleep."

"Would you like to hear the story of Big Seal?"

Jon woke up and remained motionless. Not only because

he felt an icy stab of fear when he noticed Danny had disappeared, but also because of the scene that surrounded him. Scattered icebergs floated wearily in the sea, the sky clear and bright like a sincere smile—only instead of a smile, the sun shined cheerfully. Best of all, the black no longer stained the ocean. Gone, as if it never existed. The only traces were small black stains on the edge of the ice floe and Jon's fur, still almost completely coated in the oily substance. But he could not enjoy the beauty of the scene because Danny was missing which brought the realization he was alone. That frightened him more than anything. The silence surrounding him made him uneasy and he felt panic rising in his throat.

Danny, where are you? Please come, thought Jon, crawling weak across the ice. Crossing to the edge of the iceberg, he gazed at the sea. His trembling bark echoed over the calm surface just to be lost high in the air. His black eyes filled with tears extinguishing the light of life in them, the weak light of life that barely flickered as it would soon die.

He almost fell into the sea from fear and the sudden

rush of joy when he saw Danny surfacing right in front of him to throw him a fish he caught. His whole world lit up with happiness, the feeble light flamed up brightly with renewed energy. He was too excited even to bark a greeting to his brother. His throat tightened.

"Jon, you should see the fish here." Danny whooped. "Countless schools of them."

He dove under again only to reappear with another fish which he threw to a bewildered Jon.

"Why aren't you eating?" Danny shook his head and looked at his brother. "Try them, they're good."

"Well," Jon said uncertainly, "what about you? Aren't you hungry?"

"Don't worry about me. I had enough food while you slept." Danny grinned and patted his full stomach with his flippers. "Now I have to feed you, and as soon as you're feeling better, we're off to look for our group. All right?"

"It's a deal." Jon smiled and began to eat.

The heap of fish in front of Jon grew faster than he could eat.

"Danny, slow down, I can't eat any more."

"Just this one," Danny said before diving under water.

And then again, more fish.

"Danny, I really can't. I'll burst!"

"This is the last one, I promise."

"But—"

"The last one!" Danny continued in a gentle voice, "For my baby brother."

"Oh, Danny." Jon sighed.

Danny dived into the depths of the sea, going deeper than before, much deeper. The light grew dim and he plunged further and further down. The sea teemed with plankton and other living creatures around him.

He halted to look up toward the surface of the sea from where the light silently descended slipping closer to him. It outlined clearly everything moving in the water, even the smallest sign of life in that part of the sea. Quick, like a cold gust of north wind, Danny pounced on his prey. *For my baby brother.* Surfacing, he threw it toward Jon.

"Look, Jon, look at this fish!"

Danny lost his balance and fell back into the water,

crashing flat on the surface. He sank fast and deep, the air expelling from his lungs. Dizzy and confused, he managed to come up again. But it was too late. A large white polar she-bear was hungrily devouring Jon's lifeless body.

"Jon, Jon. . . ."

But Jon no longer heard him.

"Run, Jon. . . . Run for the rainbow. . . ." Danny ran around in anguish looking for the rainbow, but there was no rainbow in the sky. "Run for the rainbow, Jon."

Choking on his tears and salty seawater tinged with Jon's blood, Danny dived into the depths. Deep down— away from the presence and the sight that would haunt him for the rest of his life. Away from reality and toward the distant world where he would hide in its bowels until the pain subsided. Where darkness and eternal silence confronted life and light, where everything was dead or appeared so, where memories faded and sank into oblivion. Deeper and deeper. Into nonexistence. . . .

*

Icebergs gradually dispersed. Each moved in a different direction, carried by sea currents, until all of them resembled solitary travelers moving slowly toward their destination.

A pitiful small body lay prostrate on an ice floe that seemed to float to nowhere in particular. Racked by sudden fits of shivering and haunted by feverish dreams, the little seal softly whined.

"Why can't you see the rainbow, Jon? Why? Run for it! You were a good seal, there must be a rainbow for you! Look around and you'll find it. Jon!"

Mom, there's no rainbow! None at all! Jon didn't find his rainbow! The rainbow doesn't exist. It doesn't exist! Why did you lie to me, Mom? Why did you tell me all those stories? Because I was a baby? Why didn't you tell me the truth when I grew up? Why, Mom? Why-y? Mo-m!

Danny woke up with a cry, hot and feverish. Glancing around, he realized it really happened. Jon was gone. Forever. Mom and his entire group were far away. He was alone, completely alone. With only this ice floe and his terrible grief.

He mourned for Jon. All the more because he blamed himself for his death. If he hadn't been so over-confident and gone after that fatal fish, Jon would be alive. And still be with him now. Their group far ahead, the brothers would continue the traveling north, to-gether. And they would have caught up to them. Even-tually. They fell behind before. Soon they would have again joined their mother. And admire the easy-going simplicity of Danny's father in a role of a superior leader, fearless and bold. Everything would be as it ought. And the boys would grow up together on the coasts beneath the cliffs of birds screaming above their heads, in the land of their fathers where the lazy sun rarely sets. Eve-rything fine . . . and Jon would. . . .

He remembered giving his brother the first fish Danny ever caught. His glossy silvery-gray fur glistened in the sunshine when he surfaced and presented him with his gift. Jon looked at him with his warm eyes and gratefully rubbed his nose against Danny's wet fur. They had so much love and understanding between them. He thought of how he encouraged insecure Jon and taught him to dive and hunt. He recalled their races, games, conversations. With remorse, he relived the moment when he left his baby brother alone while playing hide-and-seek. Then, man came putting Jon in danger. Another time Danny had not been there to help him. Fortunately, nothing happened back then, but now. . . .

Guilt gnawed at him like a marine worm and it seemed as if it would not let go.

It felt as if he had frittered his life away. If he were to die now, what would he leave behind? The dead body of his dear brother and friend, perished despite learning his lessons, despite all his knowledge of this world. What was the point, if everything you were taught and prepared for could be nullified in a single moment of carelessness? Or turned out to be false?

Danny no longer knew what to believe in, or what was true. He realized the rainbow did not exist—at least not the rainbow from the tale of Big Seal. Probably a tale simply fabricated and passed down for generations. But why? Why lie to youngsters? Danny wondered whether the story of his little sister Mary Jane were true. The little sister killed by man. . . .

On an early, misty morning, a ship arrived and disembarked men. All the seals ran away. All, except the young. Unprotected, unaware of the danger, they innocently waited for human beings to approach. A man lifted a club and struck the fragile little head. One, two, three times. Blood spattered the white fur. No cries, no sound. Silent and quick. And then again. One, two, three dull thuds, blood and death. Still, no cries. Only a blank look of surprise and disappointment. . . . Other human beings approached from the opposite side and took the surviving pups in their arms. But the men armed with rifles and clubs snatched the pups from them, bashing their skulls. One, two, three. Blows. Blood. Death. More humans came. They took away those trying to protect the pups with their bodies. Putting them on their ship, they towed it away. The remaining men skinned the bodies and loaded the furs in their ship. Leaving behind the less than two-week-old pups' corpses, they disappeared into the fog, as suddenly as they arrived. Mary Jane was among the dead pups. Frozen remains of her tiny body eerily lay motionless on the bloodstained ice with other pups killed that day. The day when humans cruelly murdered an entire generation. Wiped out. No pup left alive.

That year of the great trouble, the group set out on their northbound journey fourteen weeks earlier. Tormented by pain and grief, they listlessly went on, but there was no joy in their lives. It took them a year to recover from the shock, two years for life to return to their group and new pups to be born again. And it was all man's fault. That same being that smiled at him, caressed his fur and softly whispered to him. Man, you stayed away from because sooner or later he would be the death of you. Man, who feeds on pain and the suffering of others. Man, Danny had come to love. . . .

Carried by gentle currents on the ice floe gradually melting away, Danny sank into despondency. With every hour, every minute, he grew more miserable. Overcome with memories, he mostly slept, only opening his eyes to check the horizon for any sign of life. Then he closed his eyes again to return to his brother Jon. His whole life seemed to unfurl in his mind's eye for the umpteenth time—moments of happiness and sorrow. Jon was everywhere, sharing them with him. In time, dreams of Jon grew so strong they obliterated everything else, including the images of his father and mother. The human female with the sunshine in her hair also faded and seemed unreal. Jon, though dead and gone, became Danny's only companion.

The ice melted in the warm gusts of wind and currents growing warmer. Slightly gurgling, cold rivulets flew into the sea. Its temperature gently but steadily rising, fresh droplets glistened under the reflecting rays of the sun. Danny felt the change taking place around him. He knew something unusual was happening but paid it little attention. He didn't care. Couldn't be bothered. He only wanted to sleep and think of nothing. Just live, without any questions or obligations. Or perhaps die. . .

.

A strange noise above him in the sky, a sharp cry, a flutter of wings unknown to him, forced open his eyes. Vaguely familiar, he knew deep down he had seen a similar bird, and he wasn't dreaming. White as a cloud, the bird circled above him in the sunlit sky and at moments hid the sun. Sometimes it plunged, only to soar high into the air again. Screeching, the bird repeated the ritual several times and flew away. Left alone on his rapidly melting ice floe with the sea washing over him, Danny's memories and hunger gnawed at him. He had no strength to move and search for food. He could not be bothered. If Jon were here, maybe. But now?

The bird returned. The tiny dot on the horizon turned into a seagull that circled above Danny and what was left of his ice floe. He wondered at the snowy whiteness of its feathers, almost as white as those of the bird carrying a branch in its beak flying under the rainbow. Yes, almost as white. . . .

The seagull screeched, flapped its wings several times and again disappeared in the distance, turning into a tiny dot on the horizon.

*

When the seagull landed on the top mast, people still sang on the deck and the sound of guitar reached upward. From his place of observation, he looked down on the group having fun. The white sails, stretched like taut strings, swelled in the wind, sometimes blocking the view. The bird screeched, but none of the singers paid attention. It took off again to fly around the ship.

Smiling at the boys, she rose and walked to the prow. She already noticed the bird that kept circling around them, disappearing on the horizon and then tirelessly returning only to repeat the same ritual again. For a minute she thought the bird mistook their vessel for a fishing trawler. But the persistent bird seemed to try to attract someone's attention. She decided something else must be the matter. Standing on the prow, she shaded her eyes against the sun, looked toward the horizon. She saw nothing unusual except the seagull letting out shrill cries and flapping his wings. The bird seemed to look straight at her before vanishing into the sun-drenched expanse.

She started for the cabin on the command bridge.

"Erwin, may I please borrow the binoculars?" she

asked the young man behind the helm.

"Why, did you spot something interesting? Or just want to enjoy the view?" The young man with a face overgrown with beard gave her a wink.

He removed the binoculars over his head, readjusted his knitted snowboarding cap and pulled it a little over his eyes. He looked back at the vast expanse of the high seas, still retaining the small grin at the corners of his chapped lips.

"I'm not sure." The girl paid no attention to his sarcastic remark.

She didn't hold it against him. Just like him, she had enough of the sea, too. Their feet cried for a solid footing.

"In fact, I'm interested in a seagull. I've been watching him for some time now and it seems to me he's trying to attract our attention."

Erwin looked at her in surprise, and started to laugh.

"Ours or *yours alone*? My poor Helen, you've been on the sea so long even the seagulls make eyes at you. Mother Nature felt the desperation of its child, and sent you a feathery friend for comfort."

"I'm sure if we're lucky before we return to the base, we'll find someone for you, too. My female intuition tells me I'm not the only one who's desperate on this ship," she quipped.

Erwin laughed again, but this time his laughter sounded artificial and not as confident.

"Dream on!"

"Don't be so sure. We still have quite a journey before us."

When she opened the door, the wind carried away the delicate fragrance of her perfume and brought the smell of sea salt. As she walked off to the prow, the young man followed her with his eyes through the misty porthole. The air inside the cabin settled, filled with his longing.

The screech of the seagull prodded him into consciousness again. Although the bird was irritating, Danny could not help liking it a little. He repeated the circling ritual and then the seagull flew away to wherever he came from.

Danny pulled up, folded his flippers under his body and gazed at the tiny speck that shimmered on the horizon.

"Erwin!" She ran into the cabin, brimming with excitement. "Look, look over there!"

"What is it now, have you found another admirer?" He lifted the binoculars to his eyes. "What is it I'm supposed to see?"

"Can you see it?" she pointed with her index finger. "Something seems to be floating on the sea!"

"*Where?* I can't see anything." He scanned the sea.

"Give them to me." She grabbed the binoculars from him and focused on a particular spot. "There! At about eleven o'clock."

"Hey, easy does it! You're going to break my nose!" He took the binoculars she shoved into his face and started to survey the sea again.

"Have you found it?"

"Nothing. . . . Wait! I think I saw something, but it was gone in an instant. Like it sank or something." Confused, he scratched his head under the cap. "But what could sink *here*? We're in the middle of the ocean!"

"Erwin," she said in a pleading voice, "could we go closer and have a look? I've been haunted by a feeling that something would happen, and something tells me it's happening right now."

"I don't know." He searched the depth of her eyes. "I'm not sure. . . . We should discuss it with the others first."

"Please!" She squeezed his forearm. "Nobody will notice if we make a slight detour, particularly now." She nodded in the direction of the singing and laughter coming from the deck. "If we find nothing, if I'm wrong, we'll come back and continue as if nothing happened. Why should we disturb them for no good reason? It'll be our little secret, okay?" she whispered the last words leaning into him, close enough he felt her warm breath on his face. He got goose pimples on his neck, and was glad he wore a turtleneck sweater so Helen wouldn't notice.

"Have you ever been told you're a type of person who's highly inconvenient to have around?" Erwin said gravely. "Especially at times like this, when we're all dead tired and can hardly wait to—"

"What type?"

"Someone you can't say *no* to." He smiled at her and was rewarded by a loud kiss.

"You are a darling, Erwin. And, for the record, you're the type a woman simply cannot do without sometimes."

"I wonder whether you'll say that once we are on the land."

Helen did not hear him. Leaning against his shoulder, she stared into the distance, trying to find any sign of life. Out there, at sea.

Danny could not tell from where the seagull came back

and forth. Another ice floe or perhaps land? Although near land for a long time, he never really saw it.

Regardless of everything, and whether or not it was a chance to save himself or merely an illusion, he had to start swimming. The melting ice could not hold him anymore. Beginning to sink, Danny had nothing else he could do but set out once again on a long journey into the unknown.

He swam slowly, rolling with the waves, floating. Weak and exhausted, he kept sinking under the surface, but he did not give in. He followed his seagull.

His numbed senses sprang to life in a storm of sensations similar to a polar blizzard. Even when he had to summon all his strength to keep afloat, he needed neither the seagull nor the sun to guide him. He pushed on, driven by a surge of reawakened love. Not even the *wall of death* appearing in front of him could stop him. Fighting to the end, he rushed closer and closer to his living vision.

*

"For God's sake, Erwin, there's something going on there."

"Where?"

This time he grabbed the binoculars from her.

"Where did you see it?" he said, forgetting his manners.

"About half a mile directly in front of us."

For several long moments, he stood motionless as a stone sculpture. Then he lowered the binoculars and turned to Helen.

"Tell Brian and Fabrice . . . no, let them stay here. Find Chris and Dylan and tell them to lower the Viking and get going. You know where to."

Helen did not move at all. She stood stiff in place, anxiety and tension reflected in her eyes.

"What is it? What's the matter?" the young man said nervously, staring at the girl who appeared to try to tell him something.

She did not succeed. No need anyway, Erwin understood her mute plea.

"All right, you can go with them, just hurry up, please!"

When the net caught, embracing him, it dragged him toward the bottom. He thought he collided with an iceberg, not noticing the threatening *wall of death* that trailed in the sea, discarded. Something captured him, wrapped around his flippers and cut into his neck. Crushing him. Suffocating him. He felt dizzy, a cloudy haze in front of his eyes blotted out the bubbles floating to the surface. No matter how hard he thrashed, he could not break free of the net's deadly grip.

In the brief moment he surfaced, he thought he heard a familiar sound. Rumbling, buzzing, splashing. Dragged under too soon, he could not figure it out.

But he had managed to breathe in some air before it yanked him below the surface again. He began to hallucinate. Images floated in front of his eyes. His mother, his father, Jon, other seals. They all smiled at him. All of them except the human female with golden hair and the sea colored eyes. In hers, this time, he only saw fear.

Light as a snowflake dancing in the air, he hovered, soared high. Thrilled to float higher and higher. Smooth and effortless. Think it and you are already lifting. He longed to tell Mom and Jon about the feeling, how happy it made him. He wanted his father to be as proud of him as when he fearlessly stood face to face with a raging young seal. If only his father could see how strong his Danny became and how his sheer willpower affected life's events—of life itself. He hoped he could hold on a little longer to the last bubbles of air he unwillingly had to exhale. If only he had more time to look at the waves with the reflection of the human female into whose arms he rushed. If only he could stop the clock so everything stood still for a while.

That moment stretched into eternity. Then burst and disintegrated. Bathed in sunlight, like the white dove that flew above him carrying a twig in her beak, it was the last thing Danny saw, before meeting his rainbow.

I do not doubt I have a big heart and burning desire, but is that enough for a person to become a Rainbow Warrior, or is there something higher in us, something better? Something that lies hidden deep in our innermost selves, something only some of us manage to express and turn into what we have long missed—humanity.

Rainbow Warriors

Once again I open the pages of my diary, wishing and hoping that this is the last I write of this journey.

Since I am still badly shaken by the recent event, my observations will be more emotional than is customary on such occasions. The consequence of the awesome journey we undertook and one which all of us now can hardly wait to come to an end. We desperately need rest, although nobody wants to admit it.

The guys were fantastic, I must hand it to them, and I don't really know if I fit into their amazing company. Did I reach their standards, fulfill their and my own expectations or was I simply a disappointment? One thing I'm sure of though, after everything we've been through together, I am still not their equal. I wonder if

I'll ever be.

I do not doubt I have a big heart and burning desire, but is that enough for a person to become a Rainbow Warrior, or is there something higher in us, something better? Something that lies hidden deep in our innermost selves, something only some of us manage to express and turn into what we have long missed—humanity.

Less than half an hour ago we took from the sea yet another victim of the wall of death. *How many of them are there? One thousand, two thousand? I'm afraid it's not the last one. (Is there an end to all this?!)*

Pagophilus groenlandicus (P.G.), *which translated from Latin means the ice-lover from Greenland, about nineteen weeks old. What can one say? Too much suffering and bad luck for the weak shoulders of this poor little pup.*

1) Death caused by the irresponsibility of (local?) fishermen who have not been a threat to this species before. (Upon arrival to the base, report to Dave that trawler nets are now used in this part of the Atlantic Ocean.)

2) This is the first P.G. found so far south from the species' usual habitat that it is almost incredible.

3) The body covered in oil stains. (We have to collect data on possible oil spills that recently occurred in the waters of the North

Atlantic. That may be the cause of the seal's poor condition before his arrival to this area—his loss of orientation, physical and psychical malfunction which must be studied on the base).

Fate (man) has not been kind to this small inhabitant of Greenland. Nor to many other seals, dolphins, sea birds, turtles, whales and other mammals which are perhaps, at this very moment, dying in terrible pain, caught in one of the abandoned trawler nets. Trawler nets used by man. . . .

Time will show whether we were right or not, whether we raised such an outcry in vain and whether it was really necessary to shock the world with heart-rending reports and photographs, to upset the daily routine of ordinary people, disturbing their time for rest and their recreational habits, or spoiling their freshly-cooked meal. I can only hope that one day we shall be forgiven if it turns out that man is responsible for the extinction of the last inhabitant of the seas, and the walls of death *on their ghostly routes come to clutch us all in their deadly suffocating grip.*

I shall stop writing for a moment. Erwin is coming and, if I'm not mistaken, he seems to be bringing me a mug of steaming coffee. I admit I need it with the yearning of an addict.

*

He knocked and said from the doorway, "Hi, I brought you some coffee to warm you up." Erwin smiled tenderly. "May I come in?"

"Sure." She motioned for him to come in, closing her diary with the words *Rainbow Warrior* written on the cover. "Thank you. You're really good at guessing what one needs."

"Really?" his pearl-white teeth flashed in the semi-dark cabin. "Actually, I wanted to ask if you'd care for a stroll on the deck?"

"Of course, it's a lovely evening."

"How are you, Helen?" His back to the setting sun, he rested his hands on the railing.

"I remember better days." She avoided his gaze.

"Yeah. What happened today upset you, didn't it?"

She sipped a swallow of strong coffee and shook her head. "No. Well, a little. The truth? I didn't expect we'd come across something like—"

"Almost right at our doorstep?"

She nodded.

"Neither did I. It helps to think about something nice at such moments. A song that makes you happy, something nice that happened to you, or someone dear to you. Anything that'll work as an antibiotic against melancholy. As a kid, if I scraped my knee or elbow on a skateboard and came home in tears wailing so everyone in the neighborhood could hear me, my nana used to sit me in her lap, wash and treat my wound and tell me a story. Unfortunately, she isn't around anymore, so I have to manage on my own."

"Well, neither are you a kid," Helen said after a short break. A barely recognizable smile lit up her face.

"Exactly. And my skateboard's also history." He uttered a laugh. "I'd like to tell you something, if that's okay with you."

She shrugged—a tacit sign for him to carry on.

"This Inuit legend is about a boy who lived many, many years ago. With two twin sisters and a four years older brother, he was the youngest member of the first family that came on the southwestern coasts of Greenland. They formed an Inuit community we know today as Greenlanders, or Kalaallit. The boy in the legend possessed an unusual lively disposition and was enchanted with nature and the wildlife. He learned from his father to respect nature and live by obeying its laws—because nature was his second mother—and to kill animals only for food or clothing. Otherwise, the spirit of the slain animal would rise against its killer, bringing incalculable consequences to his family and himself as well. The boy took his father's advice to heart. Until he was eleven years old, he accompanied his father and his older brother when they hunted. He learned to stalk, kill animals and how to put to best use meat and other parts of their bodies. On days when men in his family didn't go hunting, they built houses and tents. Then he took his harpoon and hunted alone. Better to say, he only pretended to hunt while playing a game.

"One such day, the boy's father and older brother went to the neighboring family to meet other men with whom they planned to go fishing. They didn't bring the boy along because he was too young. Deeply saddened and hurt, he took off by himself. He searched, guided by his hunting instinct, for a group of seals he spotted a few days before while hunting with his father. Swinging his harpoon and wrapped in a caribou's skin around his waist, he swiftly scouted around, closing in on the group of seals. Never before that day had he seen such animals. That explained how his curiosity pushed him into this adventure. Fascinated, he stole up on one large seal lying alone behind a rock, away from the other animals. Sneaking up on him, he pretended to throw a weapon at the animal and take his life away. He played his game a couple of times changing positions, all the while being careful the big seal didn't spot or smell him. Encouraged, he approached the seal hiding behind the rocks covered with moss and sea grass. Lifting his harpoon, he aimed and pretended to throw it at the seal. At one point, a big, strong wave crashed into the rocks. The boy slipped, losing his balance, while the harpoon catapulted from his hand heading directly at the seal. The boy fell on his knees bloodying them, and the cold sea salt painfully bit into his wounds. But the moment he stood up again, he forgot about the pain that shook his body. His gaze stopped on the seal lying motionless on his side. The body of the seal was covered with blood while the boy's harpoon protruded from the heavily bleeding wound on his neck. With tentative steps, the boy approached the animal whose life died away. He remembered his father's words:

'Respect animals, for they are our brothers. They provide us with food, they give us clothes to cover our bodies and help us to build our homes. Treat them with humility and never slay them from sheer fun. Inuits do not do that.'

'What will happen if an animal is killed, but not for food?'

'Its spirit can't leave its body in peace, so it'll seek revenge. If not from the one who took its life, then certainly from one of his offspring. Therefore, Brave Warrior, listen to the wise words of the old people and never challenge the spirits. Live in peace with them and you'll have a happy life.'

"So Brave Warrior who broke the wise words of the old people took a painful and hasty walk back to his village. With his eyes brimmed with tears, he forgot about the harpoon he left protruding from the dead seal's body. All he could think of was the reproach and punishment he would get from his father once he found out what happened. Tempted to tell his father a lie, the boy pondered the plan to make up a convincing story he could present to him as the truth. At that moment, a terrible roar thundered the sky and the earth beneath him started to shake. Startled, the boy stumbled again and almost fell, but he regained his balance and wheeled around. The roar that resembled the grief of his tribe came from the same direction from which he ran. An unusual light rose to the sky from the place where the dead body of the slain seal lay. Though scared to death, Brave Warrior admitted to himself this was the most beautiful sight he had ever seen in his young life. All the summer colors of green Greenland strewn with flowers rose in several arcs toward the sun slowly disappearing behind the dark and leaden cold sky.

"The boy's heart beat madly in his chest when it dawned on him he was witnessing the life of a being— killed by his own hand—leaving this world and moving to afterlife. He also became aware of the coldness descending onto the earth, as well as the strange water that, for the first time ever, started to fall from, until then, the always smiling and friendly skies. Droplets, as sharp as rocks on which he cut himself, pricked his body. Still, he kept gazing at the rainbow that started to lose its colors and darken. Accompanied by the loud cry of seals and the cold that turned everything into ice. Spellbound, he listened to the message of Big Seal, whose spirit told him about the genesis and the purpose of existence in this world. After that the rainbow disappeared from the sky.

"When Brave Warrior regained his senses, the world around him was all white. White, strange, and cold. Never before had the boy seen it like this, but he wasn't unfazed. Guided by the spirit of Big Seal, he returned to the spot where, only a while ago, lay the body of the seal he had killed. Now it stood empty. His palms smeared with blood, he dug up the snow, found his harpoon and lifted it high above his head, as a vow, where the rainbow disappeared. Expressing gratitude to the spirit for sparing his life, he went to see his tribe. Before he continued to his new—just found—mission, he had to tell his father what had happened, bid farewell to his brother and sisters, and offer comfort to his mother for she would not see him again. Now he owed his life to the spirit of Big Seal. A new life lay before him, a new path to where the spirit would lead him for the rest of his earthly life. The truth was, the boy could have fared much worse.

This is only how Brave Warrior died, while under the rainbow a new child was born."

Erwin's eyes refocused on the present. "Helen, the boy in this legend was the first Rainbow Warrior to walk this planet. We were named after him."

She watched him bleary-eyed, mindless of where she was or the cup of coffee she held in the grip of her fingers that turned blue.

Then she wistfully smiled at him and said, "I think the legend about Rainbow Warriors is a bit different, but thank you anyway."

"There are legends and legends, Helen, and this one's mine. It can be yours too if you want. As long as Rainbow Warriors—no matter from which story, fable or legend—live among us, there is hope for this world. And even for this poor thing we came too late to save. If we believe there's a rainbow, maybe his death wasn't as terrible as it looks to us now, or in vain."

"I'd rather not talk about the rainbow anymore, Erwin." She had to muster strength for every word she said. "I'd rather lie down and have a long sleep from which no one can wake me. No shouting at me to hurry up because everything was ready for new action and we had to get moving in a few minutes time. I'd be happy with nothing more for us to do, even if I never see the rainbow again or call myself its warrior. I'd wish I hadn't found this poor fellow and that I left believing he still carelessly went after fish in safe waters of Greenland. I think this was just a bit too much for me."

Understanding, Erwin gazed deep into her eyes that took on the color of the ever darker sea. "As long as the world and man exist, there will be work for us to do. Unfortunately. Sometimes we'll be able to do it on time and achieve success, other times we'll be too late, like today. I understand your feelings, Helen, but this does not mean we ought to give up. This doesn't mean you ought to quit. On the contrary, it wouldn't be right. Because if we give up too and never come to terms with the situation, who will provide hope to these poor things? Who will take care of them? I'm afraid, we're their only chance, Helen. You know that, don't you? I'm certain they know it, too."

"It all sounds nice and praiseworthy, Erwin. But are we really their hope for survival or exactly the opposite?

If we let them learn to trust us, it could be their end. Not everybody thinks like you and me and the guys here. There aren't enough of us and we're often powerless. We can't always be where we're needed."

"That's exactly the point! It means we have to be stronger and more determined. Courageous like Rainbow Warrior who left his father, mother, and whole family, to dedicate his life to a higher cause. We have to do our best. We have to give our maximum, and perhaps even more than that."

"But, how can a man be more than what he is? This sounds absurd. As well as impossible."

"Let me paraphrase John Donne: *Be more than man, or otherwise you are less than an ant!* Don't you think his words apply to us? We're the ones who can be more than human. We can rise above the narrow minded and overcome this human plight. We! Not only can we, we must. It is our duty, Helen."

Carried away by his speech, he did not notice that he held the girl by the arms shaking her, while her lips curled as if in spasm. Or that his voice rose more than necessary and he pushed his face much too close to her pale one. When he calmed down a little, he let her go and kissed her forehead. He smiled.

"Come on, give me that coffee. It's almost completely frozen. I'll bring you a fresh mug."

He took a mug from her hand and spilled coffee into the sea. Then he headed for the cabin on the bridge.

Trembling like a small child, Helen watched the sun sinking in a deep rose sky. It gave her golden hair a special glow. She listened to the waves wash against the ship's hull, sprinkling the deck with a fine spray. Several drops touched her face and, mingling with tears, glided into the sea. She wiped her face with the sleeve of her sweater and noticed the seagull, perched on the rail. Dignified and calm like the setting sun, the seagull silently stood guard over the motionless body spread on the deck at her feet.

Pagophilus groenlandicus.

Dedicated to Danny,

victim of human greed and ruthlessness

If you cannot find the love you are looking for—discouraged by trials and everyday soul-searching, if this world seems too cold and an anguishing place, different from the one in your dreams where you want to live, and the streets you walk on look gray, unpleasant and dead, do not despair. Be brave and keep on searching for something better, because you deserve it. Don't let anything or anyone stand in your way. Do not allow those who spent their pathetic lives driven by egotism, selfishness and vanity try to stop you. Though some will laugh and make fun of you, do not be idle. Take another step. Once you have come so far, look for me under the rainbow. You will be surprised at what you'll find there. All the treasures and values you sought, lost among human beings, may no longer be unreachable, far, and unreal. They will appear possible, just as they do to me as I watch the distant lights of the harbor we are approaching. Lights that seemed so tiny and weak when we set out on our journey are now blinding me with their brilliance. The shiny glow I admire in the darkness of the night fills me with a new, yet unknown emotion and evokes pleasant, serene thoughts in my mind. I realized one thing: This is my home.

A Message to Man is the last part of Helen's diary on the *Rainbow Warrior* cruise and the finale of a magnificent journey that stands for human dignity and unblemished ideals.

The complete diary, published in several weekly installments in all major newspapers around the world, received considerable response from the public.

A NOTE FROM THE AUTHOR

Many things have changed since the first pioneers started their fight for the seals almost three decades ago. Previously, millions of animals were subjected to the inhumane hunt and incomprehensible suffering. Already endangered by rapid climate changes, they were mercilessly persecuted by human greed, under various pretenses.

Each spring the blood stained the beautiful landscape of Newfoundland. Hundreds of thousands—millions—of seal pups were slaughtered, some of them not any older than two weeks when they were left wounded to die in agony or drown after being skinned alive. Their cries for help shattered the pristine silence and merged with one other cry. A cry that changed the face of the world, demanded an end to the killing of baby seals.

What Greenpeace started a long time ago grew into an international movement. Animal protection and rights organizations, supported by millions of individuals from various parts of our planet, became a unified force, resolute in its demands to end the seal slaughter and the suffering of these beautiful, adorable creatures.

I was also one of them.

In 1992 I raised my voice for the first time by writing a novella *Look for Me Under the Rainbow*. Twelve years later I became actively involved in Animal Friends Croatia by campaigning for the end of the Canadian seal slaughter.

As the face of the world changed, I felt obliged to make some modifications to my book. In other words, *modernize* it to make it more appealing and contemporary.

The original story was almost left unchanged, with a few exceptions of added parts and some literary improvements. What did change, though, in comparison to its original edition, is that there are no longer photos of the seal slaughter documented by Greenpeace in it. Why is that so?

Everyone will tell you pictures speak louder than words. Absolutely true. Yet, I opted to omit these pictures from this new edition. Not because I do not appreciate what Greenpeace once did for the seals. Quite the contrary. I felt it wouldn't be fair to those other groups and individuals who from their homes in front of their computers, in the streets and squares of their towns, on the decks of their vessels, or on the cold ice of Canada fight to save those innocent lives. There are so many, and I feel enormous gratitude to and affection for each and every one of you.

All of you are heroes of our time. All of you are a part of the ever greater *community* of Rainbow Warriors who opened their eyes and their hearts to a greater cause.

Precisely because of you, I decided to let my words speak for themselves. A call to open the hearts and minds of a new Rainbow Warriors generation, to find the strength again to paint the face of this world in brighter colors. The colors of compassion, empathy, tolerance, understanding. The colors of new hope.

The colors of the rainbow.

I live with faith that this new version of my story—without pictures, but one with many images painted through words—will be worthy of your efforts and will follow and encourage you on the long path of your noble mission.

For those of you who want more information or to get actively involved, please visit some of the following links below. Thank you.

www.seashepherd.org

www.harpseals.org

www.humanesociety.org

www.ifaw.org

www.peta.org

www.greenpeace.org

www.animal-friends-croatia.org

"The Sea Shepherd Conservation Society represents the seals—they are our clients. We speak for them. If people do not like what the seals have to say then we have no apologies for that. My description of what a young seal sees as a sealer approaches it is in fact what a seal pup sees before having his face bashed in by a club. That is a description of helplessness.

"The seals will not suffer in silence, they will not be wiped out in a vacuum of apathy. They will be heard even if we have to outrage an entire nation."

—Captain Paul Watson, founder of Greenpeace and
Sea Shepherd Conservation Society

Did you like my story? If your answer is yes, please connect with me and follow me via my linktr.ee/bernardjan. Say hi and I promise I'll respond.

Please continue reading now and find bonuses you may like.

ACKNOWLEDGEMENTS

I want to thank my beta readers Susan Cava and Thomas Carley Jr. for their valuable input on this English edition, Trish Reeb, for her great editing and patience with me; and my loving parents Ksenija and Dubravko, for believing in Danny from the start.

I am grateful to my designer Mario Kožar MKM Media for creating another great cover for my books and Anita Euschen as my overall support. Many thanks to Jonathan Hill for helping me with my blurb as he had also done with *A World Without Color.*

I can't forget Angel Ramon Medina who again

answered my endless questions and Derek Doepker for being my motivator and coach.

So many people helped me with comments and input during the publishing process. I can't thank you enough for that, but I will show you my gratitude once *Look for Me Under the Rainbow* has been launched.

SHARE WHAT YOU LOVE
(ABOUT THE AUTHOR)

If you liked my writing and enjoyed reading *Look for Me Under the Rainbow*, I invite you to visit my website bernardjanofficial.wixsite.com/bernardjan where you may, if you like, subscribe to my mailing list and join my other friends, readers and supporters.

While you're there, I encourage you to also check out my other books: *Postcards From Beyond Reality: The Selected Poems of Michael Daniels*, *Cruel Summer*, *January River*, and *A World Without Color*. And I hope you'll take time to read my blog Muse. I'm honored and grateful for your support.

I'm also an animal rights advocate and environmentalist. If you like what you read here and on my website, connect with me and follow me on my favorite social networks via my linktr.ee/bernardjan.

There is no greater joy than to share what you love with those who appreciate it.

Thank you,

BJ

REVIEWS

Thank you for reading *Look for Me Under the Rainbow*. Please consider leaving an honest review on Amazon and Goodreads. It doesn't have to be long. Even a sentence or two makes a huge difference and will be much appreciated.

Indie authors depend on you. You're the reason why we write and publish.

Your honest review generates a beacon of light to other readers seeking books to enjoy. One that takes them elsewhere as they get lost between the pages.

Thank you for that. Thank you for sharing our

stories.

Please also leave your honest review for *A World Without Color*, *January River*, *Cruel Summer*, and *Postcards From Beyond Reality: The Selected Poems of Michael Daniels* on Amazon.

ONE STORY. TWO ENDINGS. GENUINE AND FICTIONAL.

WHICH ENDING IS YOURS?

BERNARD JAN

A WORLD WITHOUT COLOR
A TRUE STORY

POWERFUL. EMOTIONAL. HONEST.

ACCLAIM FOR

A WORLD WITHOUT COLOR

"This short powerful novella is a must read. It gave me permission to stop grieving in many ways, because Bernard Jan told me it was okay to feel like I did and it was okay to move on, despite suffering an emptiness that will never be filled. I would give this book to anyone who has pets, because it will give you an insight into what will happen one day. We're telling you it is okay and that you aren't alone."

—Haley Jenkins, owner of Selcouth Station Press

"As someone who has worked with hospice, in hospital, health care centers, and survivor's of loss and trauma, for close to 40 years, I must say that this is one of the most honest, compassionate, and understanding descriptions of what grief can feel like that I have ever read—and I've read a lot of books about grief, loss, death and bereavement."

—Gabriel Constans, author of over fifteen books and
screenwriter

"Bernard Jan chronicles the final stage in the life of a cat named Marcel, as Bernard, his family, and Marcel face Marcel's death. The capacity for the depth of bond in an interspecies way has always amazed me. This has been illustrated to me very recently with the death of my own cat, Poppy. She was the runt of the litter, not meant to survive, smaller than my undersized palm when she arrived, but she lived for just about twenty-five years. I relay my story because this short book reflects the dilemmas and conflicted emotions faced when dealing with, and having ultimate responsibility for, the final breath of a creature greatly loved."

—Rebecca Gransden, author of *anemogram.* and *Rusticles*

"Bernard Jan has taken a piece of his own heart and soul and put down in words, his feelings, his thoughts, and the utter devastation of the raw loss of his beloved pet."

—Dianne Bylo, review writer for Tome Tender

"If you're looking for a sad story then this is for you . . . I felt that I was Bernard at the end of the book, I love books that pull me in and make me feel that I'm part of the book. You'll have to read it for yourself to experience this."

—Angel Ramon Medina, author of *The Thousand Years War Series*, *Angel's Nightmare Adventure Series* and *Janus: The Devil's Election*

"Bernard Jan's novella is guaranteed to evoke powerful

emotions in the reader. More than once I was reading the words through the fog of my own tears. This is not only due to the compelling theme of unconditional love, but can also be attributed to the author's poetic use of language which help to garner these feelings. His descriptions and thoughts are beautiful and moving. From the joyful flashbacks to the inevitable death of Marcel, the scenes are completely enchanting."

—Leonard Tillerman, educator and freelance writer

"Bernard Jan does a marvelous job of making this story personal—not just for him, since this is indeed a true account of the end of a love story—but for ourselves, the readers, which will have to feel what he feels with a strength that's sometimes overpowering . . . The writing is beautiful and direct, and clicks immediately . . . Story and feelings aside, I love how the author touched on topics such as animal abuse, veganism, and so many others that should really be more prominent in our life, but that alas, are relegated to the random thought every now and then."

—Dario Cannizzaro, author of *On Life, Death, Aliens and Zombies* and *Dead Men Naked*

"Bernard Jan walks readers through his sorrow with unusual sensitivity and insight. His emotions are palpable, and I was caught up in his sorrow, watching his pet slowly die, unable to prevent its passing. This short novella is beautifully written and easy to read, leaving me pondering the fleeting nature of time and life."

—Stefan Vucak, writer of over fifteen contemporary drama and SF novels, editor and book reviewer

"This book is well written and spoken from the heart. You can feel Bernard's pain with every word, feel the love he has for this cat who is so much more the just the family pet. The book cover needs no words, all the love and emotion are right there."

—Linda Thompson, host of TheAuthorsShow.com

"Reading this book, I got a glimpse of something I never had with a pet. Bernard Jan's writing flows that you don't have force yourself to read someone's most inner feelings. His book shines a light on my humanity, and I question my dependency on eating meat. How do we face the certain death of a loved one? Bernard does it with emotion and honesty and most importantly with originality."

—Damien Black, author of *Life of a Bastard*

A WORLD WITHOUT COLOR EXTRACT

You curl up in your new hideout, and the soft light of the April afternoon washes your worn-out body. You are aware of my closeness. You confirm that with a gentle sigh while my palm tenderly slides down your fur. You still like my touch, although pain is what you now mostly feel. And uncertainty—but for how long?

Against the tracksuit pants I wipe a lock of your hair which is stuck to my palm. I try to take a better position, crawling next to you under the table. I hate the sentimentality of people who want to capture with photos the beautiful moments in life because they believe that's the only way they can remain part of their memories. Ironic, because I myself resort to this now. Nothing else is left for me. Another day, week, month at best is the most optimistic prognosis.

Only this time. I will make an exception.

Your chest is rising and falling, fighting for every breath. It's not easy for you, I know, and I would love most if I could breathe for you. But I can't. Even if I breathe a new life into you, it probably wouldn't help. You wouldn't even let me. Because you are a fighter. Besides, it seems to me you don't like people taking pity on you, as you didn't like it when they laughed in your face. This is why I control myself when I'm around you, poorly disguising the true nature of my feelings in a lame attempt to preserve your dignity. Panic hits me because of what is coming!

A tidal wave rushes from within, forcing tears to my eyes, which stream silently down my face and drip-drop onto your colorful blanket. Jolly green, purple and beige squares support your long, thin and distorted body like a gentle cloud. The shadow of what you used to be.

I support myself on my elbows, taking the first

snapshot with my cell phone in my left hand. You hear a click and crack open your eyes. Your gaze rests on me, warming me with the heat of the hearth fire that fades away. I take another picture, producing another click, and then my hand trembles; I have to dry the tears that, undecided, stop and pause in the corners of my eyes.

You raise your head, not ceasing to look at me. Your good eye caresses my soul, while the other, sick from cataracts and inflammation unsuccessfully treated with ointments and drops, looks into the unknown. I'm stroking your hair, matted around it, waiting for you to be ready to continue our little photo session.

Again you accept me and indulge my whim. Gently as a newborn, you push your head along my hand, responding to my caress. First you rub your little nose into my fingers, and then you push your left ear against my hand, wanting me to scratch and massage it. When you become bored or you think it is enough, with amazing vigor you start to wash yourself. You surprise me a little because I don't remember when was the last time I saw you wash yourself. (It was a long time ago, just as eons have gone by since the days when you would happily nestle in the most comfortable seat in the apartment, after successfully sponging an abundant meal, and start to clean yourself. An invisible clock, or timer in you—as we used to joke—woke you up and led you, with your tail raised, to your bowls, where you patiently waited until, usually Mom, capitulated before your determination and persistence of the winner.) I smile, encouraged by a false hope and strong mental images awakened from the past. How little it takes for the Phoenix to resurrect in me and clatter the wings of joy. How dishonest I am with myself (and you) and subject to self-deception!

I leave you for a moment and hurry into the kitchen to show the photos to Mom. You continue sprucing up, as you know it's time for Saša's arrival. As always, you want to show yourself to him in the best light. You care about what Saša thinks of you. I don't think you do this so he can pet you and lavish words of praise on you, calling you Viola, Love. No, you accept Saša because you know you will be better each time you see him and you want to give something back to him. You want to show him that his visits really make you feel better. And so you do that. I don't know with which words I can express more clearly what I feel for you, so I will repeat: Viola, my love.

My thoughts come rushing back like raging currents of mountain rivers that do not stop for anything or anyone. Hurrying with a roar to their finish line, completely self-sufficient. Each word I make immortal here must be engraved with the dedication of a blind stonemason who, just by sense of touch and guided by indestructible faith, creates from the shapeless mass a work which present generations, but also those who come after, will admire. Those who are alive today, and their children who are just born, setting the foundation for new generations. This is our written monument and I snuggle up against it, blinded by the pain inflicted upon me by every minute that takes us into the future. The future is what I want to avoid at any cost, selfishly keeping the present so these moments last as long as possible. Not thinking about you and the relief it will bring you. We are both on the road of no return. Do you think so too? Do you also feel at least a fraction of regret we will part soon, with no guarantee and no promise that, in the blink of an eye or the distant future, we might meet each other again? Tell me, dearest. . . .

Please leave your honest review on Amazon.

www.ingramcontent.com/pod-product-compliance
Lightning Source LLC
Chambersburg PA
CBHW071957170626
46813CB00005B/1906